To Pippa Gerrett and Year Four (2004)
of Sturminster Marshall First School,
where this story began – JJ

For Suzy – with love LC

CLASS TWO AT THE ZOO

by **Julia Jarman** and **Lynne Chapman**

First published in 2007 by Hodder Children's Books
First published in paperback in 2008

Text copyright © Julia Jarman 2007
Illustration copyright © Lynne Chapman 2007

Hodder Children's Books
338 Euston Road
London NW1 3BH

Hodder Children's Books Australia
Level 17/207 Kent Street
Sydney, NSW 2000

A catalogue record of this book is
available from the British Library.

ISBN: 978 0 340 91161 7
10 9 8 7 6 5 4 3

Printed in China

Hodder Children's Books
is a division of Hachette
Children's Books.
An Hachette Livre UK Company

www.juliajarman.com
www.lynnechapman.co.uk

CLASS TWO AT THE ZOO

TICKETS

JULIA JARMAN

Illustrated by
LYNNE CHAPMAN

A division of Hachette Children's Books

Hodder
Children's
Books

They saw a giraffe having a laugh.

They didn't see...

...the anaconda.

zzzzz

They heard Teacher say,
'We must keep together!'
'Don't wander off!' and
'Watch the weather!'

They saw parrots
squabbling in the sky,
but they didn't see...

...the anaconda sigh,
and open one eye
to spy on Class Two as they
walked round the zoo.

They saw hippos **hopPing** in the mud.

They saw monkeys eating **chocolate pud.**

But they didn't see the anaconda ponder...

...then **slide** from the water
and start to wander...

...after Class Two
on their trip round the zoo,
some of them walking two by
two.

They saw spotty cheetahs running a mile.

They saw two gorillas jumPing a stile.

But they failed to see that huge reptile...

...**Open** his jaws and **swallow Kyle.**

They didn't see that **giant** snake...

...gulp down **Gerty and Anita.**

Molly turned and saw **the creature!**

'**Look out!**' she cried, – alas too late – Teacher was gone and so was **Kate!**

Well, most of **Kate** – so **Molly** was quick.

She grabbed hold of a sturdy stick.

Without a single moment's pause
she stuck it between the
monster's jaws.

'Come on!'
she urged the rest of Class Two –
as she grabbed Kate's feet –

'To the
rescue!'

The rest of Class Two all heaved and tugged...

and Gerty...

and Anita,

and Diana...

and Jake,

and James...

and Kyle –

his smile
as wide as
a crocodile!

Then a boy they didn't know.

'Thank you,' he said,

'my name is Joe.'

'Phew!' said Class Two as they fled from the zoo.

Let this be a terrible warning for you!

When you go on a safari or visit a zoo,
keep your eyes open whatever you do.

Watch out for the snake,
lying low in the lake,
and if you see the anaconda
open an eye and start to wander,
don't, even for a second, ponder...

run!